From his home on the other side of the moon, Father Time summoned eight of his most trusted storytellers to bring a message of hope to all children. Their mission was to spread magical tales throughout the world: tales that remind us that we all belong to one family, one world; that our hearts speak the same language, no matter where we live or how different we look or sound; and that we each have the right to be loved, to be nurtured, and to reach for a dream.

This is one of their stories.
Listen with your heart and share the magic.

FOR SYLVIE AND
HER UNCLE RICK,
WHOSE CAPACITY
TO LOVE HAS
AWAKENED OUR
HEARTS.

Our thanks to artists Shanna Grotenhuis, Jane Portaluppi, and Mindi Sarko,
as well as Sharon Beckett, Yoshie Brady, Andrea Cascardi, Solveig Chandler, Jun Deguchi,
Akiko Eguchi, Liz Gordon, Tetsuo Ishida, William Levy, Michael Lynton, Masaru Nakamura,
Steve Ouimet, Tomoko Sato, Isamu Senda, Minoru Shibuya, Jan Smith, and Hideaki Suda.

THE MAGIC CAP

Inspired by an Old Swedish Tale

Flavia Weedn & Lisa Weedn Gilbert

Illustrated by Flavia Weedn

Hyperion • New York

Once upon a time, a mother and her young son lived in a tiny cottage near a forest. Although they were very poor, their home was warm and filled with love.

The mother
worked very hard,
sewing for the
wealthy neighbors,
baking bread and
pies for their fancy
parties, and taking
on whatever odd
jobs they would
give her.

But at night, when her work was done, she and her son would sit by the fire, sharing stories and dreams and precious time. The boy didn't have all the toys and playthings that the neighbors' children had, but he never complained or wanted for more . . . because he knew he had something far more valuable.

One day, in the midst of a very cold winter, the mother took whatever scraps of thread and yarn she could find and made her son a cap. "This will help keep you warm when you go outside to gather wood," she said. "It is not fancy, but it is made from my heart."

The little boy was very pleased with the cap and thanked his mother over and over. He knew that she needed a cap even more than he, but he graciously accepted it because he knew how happy it made her and because he loved her so much.

Every time he put the cap on his head, he felt a strange and wonderful feeling come over him. Whatever it was, it made him feel so good inside that he decided the cap must be magic. Excitedly, he told everyone he knew.

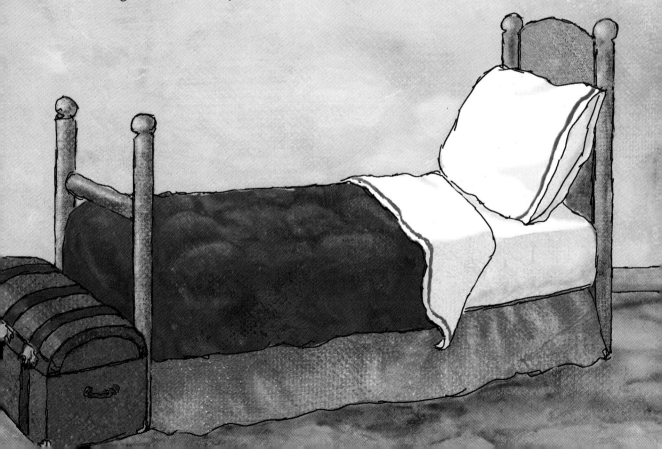

One day he decided to go for a walk in the forest. On his way he met a farmer who had already heard of the magic cap. After all, news like that travels very quickly through a forest.

"Young man, I will trade you my warm coat for your cap," the farmer said. "It is very cold and my coat will be of much more use to you than that cap."

The boy, although he needed the coat, said, "No, thank you, sir, I could never trade my cap for anything. You see, my mother made it for me."

Suddenly the farmer grabbed the cap. And, putting it on his head, he began to run away, with the boy running right after him.

Then, just as suddenly, the farmer stopped, threw the cap back to the boy, and said, "This cap is not magic! I feel nothing special when I wear it. You foolish boy, it's just an ordinary old cap!"

The boy caught
the cap and quickly
put it back on his
head. Once more,
that wonderful
feeling came over
him, and he was
happy, because he
knew the magic
hadn't gone away.

"The farmer
doesn't understand,"
he thought to
himself. "Surely he
has made a mistake.
This cap of mine,
it *is* magic!"

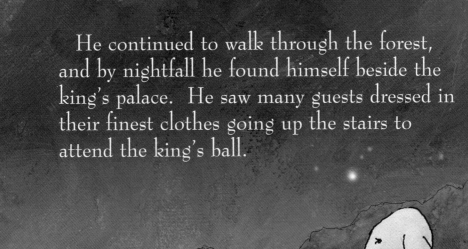

He continued to walk through the forest, and by nightfall he found himself beside the king's palace. He saw many guests dressed in their finest clothes going up the stairs to attend the king's ball.

One of the guards at the palace door, having heard of the boy's magic cap, quickly ushered him through the door and inside the palace. Once inside, the boy was noticed by the king.

When the king saw the boy's cap, he approached the boy and said, "I will trade you my crown for that magic cap." But the boy replied, "I am sorry, Your Majesty, but I cannot trade anything for my cap. You see, my mother made it for me."

"If you won't trade for my crown," the king said, "then live here in the palace so that I might sometimes wear your magic cap." But when the boy refused and tried to leave the palace, the king stopped him.

The king desperately wanted the cap—and he was used to getting everything he wanted—so he quickly ordered a servant to take the cap from the boy. The servant did so and, just as quickly, the king placed the cap upon his head. He stood there wearing the cap, but no magical feeling came over him.

Embarrassed and angry, the king ordered the boy and his cap thrown out of the palace. "You are a liar and a fraud," he shouted. "There is no magic at all in that cap!"

Crying, the boy began to run home. He was hurt and confused, and he couldn't understand why no one else could feel the magic in his cap, or why anyone would treat him so unkindly.

On his way back through the forest, the boy
was approached by a wise old woman who
asked him why he was crying. At first the boy
feared that she, too, would try to take his cap,
but her gentle ways convinced him to stop and
tell her his story.

The old woman listened, understood, and smiled tenderly. She took his hand and reassured him that the cap really was magic after all.

But the magic existed only for him. "That wonderful feeling is love," she said. "The kind of love that is known only to giving, gentle hearts."

This made the boy think of his mother, and he smiled, because he understood what the wise woman was saying. The love in his heart overflowed, and he couldn't wait to be with his mother. He thanked the old woman and ran home, holding tightly to his cap.

When at last he
arrived at the small
cottage, his mother
and a neighbor boy
were standing outside.
He ran up to his
mother, threw his arms
around her, and told her
all that had happened.
His mother smiled, just
as the wise old woman
had, but the neighbor
did not.

Instead, his neighbor said, "You fool! You fool! You could have been rich for the rest of your life if you had traded that plain old cap for the king's crown. Don't you understand? And if you had lived there in the palace with the king, you could have bought a thousand caps and had all the toys in the world."

The boy just looked at his neighbor and said, "But it is you who do not understand. The love I know my mother put into this cap, when she made it just for me, gives me such a good feeling inside . . . and that's the magic of it all. That is why no one else ever felt the magic when they tried to wear the cap.

"I could never trade it for anything," the boy continued, "and don't you see, I don't need riches and I don't need to live in a palace. I have a mother who loves me more than anything in the whole world . . . and that makes me richer than any king could ever be."

As the neighbor walked away,
the young boy hugged his mother
and she kissed him, and together
they walked to the cottage.

The little boy and his mother
had learned something their hearts
already knew . . . that the giving
of love is itself the greatest magic
of all. And that night, as they sat
by the fire to exchange stories and
dreams, the boy's cap seemed to
shimmer like gold.

Produced in cooperation with Dream Maker Studios AG.
Printed in Singapore.
For information address Hyperion Books for Children,
114 Fifth Avenue, New York, New York 10011.

FIRST EDITION
1 3 5 7 9 10 8 6 4 2

Library of Congress Cataloging-in-Publication Data

Weedn, Flavia
The magic cap/Flavia Weedn & Lisa Weedn Gilbert;
illustrated by Flavia Weedn—1st ed.
p. cm.—(Flavia dream maker stories)
Summary:A Swedish tale about a little boy whose mother makes him a cap
that seems to have magic in it, a magic that others try to steal, but cannot.
ISBN 0-7868-0119-0
[1. Fairy tales. 2. Folklore—Sweden.]
I. Gilbert, Lisa Weedn. II. Title.
III. Series: Weedn, Flavia. Flavia dream maker stories.
PZ8.W423Mag   1995
[E] 398.2'0948502—dc20   94–32814

The artwork for each picture is digitally mastered using acrylic on canvas.
This book is set in 17-point Bernhard Modern.